Dear Parents:

Congratulations! Your child is taking the first steps on an exciting journey. The destination? Independent reading!

STEP INTO READING® will help your child get there. The program offers five steps to reading success. Each step includes fun stories and colorful art or photographs. In addition to original fiction and books with favorite characters, there are Step into Reading Non-Fiction Readers, Phonics Readers and Boxed Sets, Sticker Readers, and Comic Readers—a complete literacy program with something to interest every child.

Learning to Read, Step by Step!

Ready to Read   Preschool–Kindergarten
• big type and easy words • rhyme and rhythm • picture clues
For children who know the alphabet and are eager to begin reading.

Reading with Help   Preschool–Grade 1
• basic vocabulary • short sentences • simple stories
For children who recognize familiar words and sound out new words with help.

Reading on Your Own   Grades 1–3
• engaging characters • easy-to-follow plots • popular topics
For children who are ready to read on their own.

Reading Paragraphs   Grades 2–3
• challenging vocabulary • short paragraphs • exciting stories
For newly independent readers who read simple sentences with confidence.

Ready for Chapters   Grades 2–4
• chapters • longer paragraphs • full-color art
For children who want to take the plunge into chapter books but still like colorful pictures.

STEP INTO READING® is designed to give every child a successful reading experience. The grade levels are only guides; children will progress through the steps at their own speed, developing confidence in their reading.

Remember, a lifetime love of reading starts with a single step!

Visit us on the Web!
StepIntoReading.com
randomhousekids.com

Educators and librarians, for a variety of teaching tools, visit us at RHTeachersLibrarians.com

ISBN 978-0-553-52460-4 (trade) — ISBN 978-0-553-52461-1 (lib. bdg.)
Printed in the United States of America
10 9 8 7 6 5 4 3 2 1

nickelodeon

READY TO RACE!

BLAZE AND THE MONSTER MACHINES™

Based on the teleplay "Blaze of Glory"
by Clark Stubbs

Illustrated by Kevin Kobasic

Random House 🏠 New York

Blaze is
a Monster Machine.

AJ drives Blaze.
They like to go
really fast!

Blaze and AJ zoom
to the Monster Dome.

They meet Gabby.

She has a big toolbox.

She can fix anything.

Growl!

Here comes Stripes.

He is a tiger truck.

He has claws
on his tires.
He climbs a tree!

Starla is a cowgirl truck.
She twirls her rope.

<u>Yee-haw!</u>

Starla ropes

Gabby's toolbox.

11

Darington is a stunt
truck.
He loves to do tricks.
<u>Ta-da!</u>

Zeg is a dinosaur truck.

He loves

to smash things.

Crusher is
a big truck.
He is sneaky.

Pickle is a small truck.

He is nice.

Starla asks Blaze
and AJ
to be in a race.

Blaze rolls up
to the starting line.
Ready! Set! Go!

Crusher wants to win.

He decides to cheat.

He spills oil
on the track.

Zeg and Starla

slide in the oil slick.

Crusher puts glue
on the track.
Stripes gets stuck!

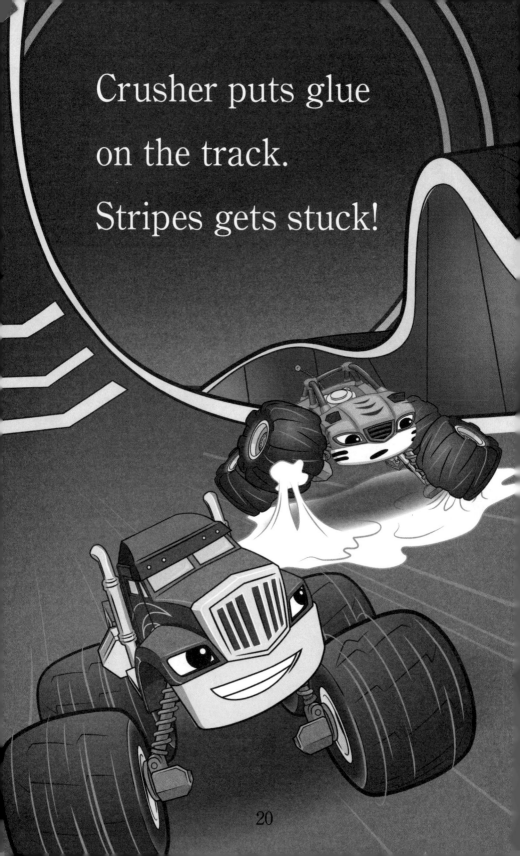

Crusher rolls balls
onto the the track.
Darington slips.
Crusher takes the lead!

Blaze is really fast.
He passes Crusher.
Crusher cannot
catch him.

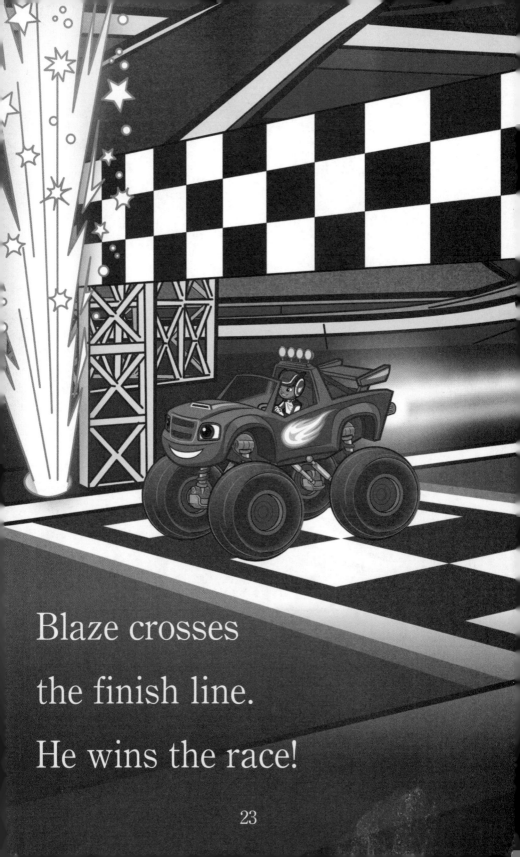

Blaze crosses
the finish line.
He wins the race!

The Monster
Machines
cheer for Blaze.
Hooray!